TWO KEYS

Volume 1
Chloe Chan and Aliena Shoemaker

D0082234

Contents of the book © 2011 Chloe Chan and Aliena Shoemaker
Published and distributed by Manga Magazine
http://www.mangamagazine.net

TWO KEYS
chapter 1: missing persons

IF THIS WERE A NOIR-DETECTIVE MOVIE, I WOULD BEGIN WITH, "IT WAS A DAY LIKE ANY OTHER DAY,"

EXCEPT THIS ISN'T A DETECTIVE MOVIE AND I'M NOT A PRIVATE INVESTIGATOR.

AT LEAST, ANYMORE.

I DIDN'T KNOW WHY I DIDN'T SEE IT COMING.

PEOPLE TEND TO LIKE THE MYSTERY THAT SURROUNDS A PRIVATE EYE, EVEN MORESO FOR A RETIRED ONE.

YOU WANT ME TO...

THEY HEAR GREATLY EXAGGERATED ACCOUNTS OF SOME EXPLOIT AND EVENTUALLY DECIDE THAT MY RETIREMENT IS DUE TO A SECRET, UNSPEAKABLE REASON

...Find this person.

THAT IS ANYTHING BUT MY DESIRE TO NOT BE A PRIVATE EYE ANYMORE.

TO BE HONEST, I WAS PASSABLE AT BEST AS A P.I. EVEN BEFORE I RETIRED.

THE JOB ITSELF IS A LOT MORE ABOUT GETTING PICTURES OF CHEATING HUSBANDS AND A LOT LESS ABOUT MURDER CONSPIRACIES,

AND THE FEW CASES I DID SOLVE WERE BY BLIND LUCK ALONE.

AFTER SEVERAL LONG STAKE-OUTS WHERE I DIDN'T QUITE MANAGE TO STAY AWAKE, A FEW LOST DOGS AND AN UNFORTUNATE INCIDENT INVOLVING CUSTARD,

I DECIDED THAT I'D HAD ENOUGH.

LUCAS BLAIRE WAS ONE OF THE MOST IMPORTANT MEN IN EXODUS,

BEING THE SON OF A POLITICIAN AND A HIGH-RANKING AFIA.

WHEN SOMEONE SO IMPORTANT GOES MISSING,

PEOPLE KNOW ABOUT IT.

IT MAKES ME UNEASY THAT I'D BEEN UNAWARE,

AND THAT I'M SUPPOSED TO FIND THIS MAN MAKES ME UNEASIER STILL.

We're trying to prevent panic in the general population, part of which includes finding him as quickly as possible.

I'm not to disclose any more information until you accept the case,

but I hope you understand the implications regarding the situation.

BOY, DO I.

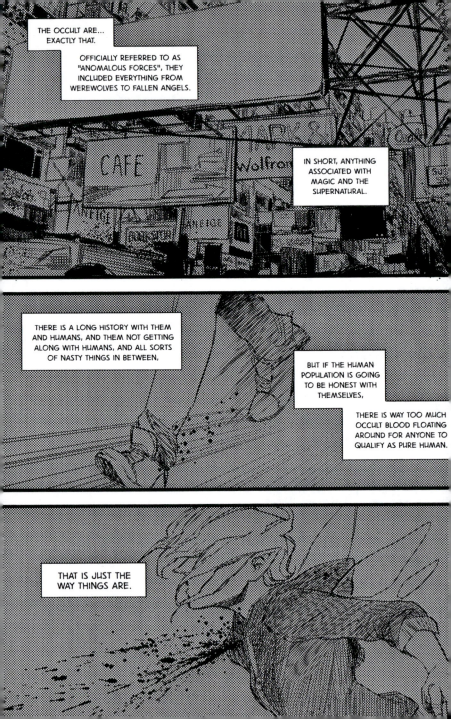

THE OCCULT ARE...
EXACTLY THAT.

OFFICIALLY REFERRED TO AS
"ANOMALOUS FORCES", THEY
INCLUDED EVERYTHING FROM
WEREWOLVES TO FALLEN ANGELS.

IN SHORT, ANYTHING
ASSOCIATED WITH
MAGIC AND THE
SUPERNATURAL.

THERE IS A LONG HISTORY WITH THEM
AND HUMANS, AND THEM NOT GETTING
ALONG WITH HUMANS, AND ALL SORTS
OF NASTY THINGS IN BETWEEN,

BUT IF THE HUMAN
POPULATION IS GOING
TO BE HONEST WITH
THEMSELVES,

THERE IS WAY TOO MUCH
OCCULT BLOOD FLOATING
AROUND FOR ANYONE TO
QUALIFY AS PURE HUMAN.

THAT IS JUST THE
WAY THINGS ARE.

THAT, HOWEVER, DOESN'T MAKE BEING AN OCCULT LEGAL.

THERE IS EVEN AN ENTIRE ORGANIZATION— THE *AFIA*, OR ANOMOLOUS FORCES INTELLIGENCE AGENCY—DEDICATED TO THE CAPTURE AND "RECTIFYING" OF THE OCCULT,

WHICH EVERYONE SUSPECTS INVOLVE DRAGGING THEM OFF TO A BASE IN SOME FLAT PLAINS AND STICKING NEEDLES INTO THEM

TO FIND OUT WHAT EXACTLY WOULD "CURE" THEM.

NO ONE CAME BACK, SO APPARENTLY THEY HAVEN'T BEEN TOO SUCCESSFUL.

CLICK

BUT I DIGRESS.

ACTUALLY, IT'S BECAUSE THE PLACE REEKED OF OCCULT, AND IT'S COMING FROM A DOWNWARD DIRECTION.

HE WAS CUT OFF.

BAD RECEPTION.

UNDERGROUND.

BUT AUDREY DOESN'T NEED TO KNOW THAT. REALLY.

WELL-PLAYED, DETECTIVE.

Hm.

WELL-PLAYED.

. . . . .

THIS IS STRANGE.

I'M SURE THAT WE NEED TO GO LOWER, BUT I CAN'T SEE A WAY DOWN ANYWHERE

There's nothing here.

I GUESS IT WAS NAIVE TO EXPECT SOMETHING THAT DIDN'T WANT TO BE FOUND OUT IN THE OPEN, AND WE'RE IN A SHOPPING MALL, AFTER ALL.

AND, ANY LOWER AND WE'D BE IN THE SUBWAY TUNNEL.

MCKENZIE PICKED JOYCE UP SEVEN YEARS AGO.

BEEN TAKIN' CARE OF 'EM SINCE.

JOYCE WAS JUST A KID, YANNO?

AND MCKENZIE WAS PRETTY MUCH A LONE WOLF BEFORE THEN.

CUE WARNING BELLS. "SEVEN YEARS AGO" IS TABOO TERRITORY.

PEOPLE LIKE TO PRETEND THAT YEAR DIDN'T HAPPEN.

HAVE ANY OF YOU MET THEM?

I DON'T LIKE WHERE THIS IS GOING ONE BIT.

SEEN 'EM AROUND. NEVER TALKED TO 'EM.

I'VE TALKED TO MCKENZIE ONCE.

SURPRISINGLY POLITE GUY, GIVEN HIS REP.

OH YEAH, THE GUY'S GOT A REP.

I HEARD HE WAS INVOLVED IN THE JINX WARS.

EVERYONE WAS.

REP?

chapter 2:
Seven Years

...LIKE
THEY'RE NOT
THERE AT ALL.

CHANGELINGS ARE OCCULT WHO HAVE A SPELL CAST ON THEM, TO GIVE THEM THE PERFECT APPEARANCE OF A HUMAN.

IT'S USUALLY USED BY OCCULT WHO DON'T ALREADY LOOK HUMAN, BECAUSE, WHY THE FUCK WOULD YOU USE IT OTHERWISE?

S A POWERFUL SPELL T HAS TO BE CAST AT BIRTH OF THE OCCULT,

AT THE COST OF THE LIFE OF A HUMAN BABY.

HEY.

Hey. Hi, Flicka.

HI.

TYPICALLY, WHAT FOLLOWS IS THAT THE OCCULT BABY IS THEN SWAPPED BACK INTO THE HUMAN FAMILY, SO IT CAN TRY TO LIVE AS A HUMAN.

THERE IT IS. CAN YOU TELL US ANYTHING?

BECAUSE, NO MATTER WHAT KIND OF SHIT FAMILY IT'S POSSIBLY STUCK WITH,

IT STILL HAS BETTER CHANCES AS A HUMAN THAN AN OCCULT.

I'M NOT SURE WHAT FLICKA ACTUALLY IS, BUT IT DOESN'T REALLY MATTER.

AS FAR AS I CAN TELL, SHE DOESN'T KNOW EITHER, NOR DOES SHE CARE.

Are you alright?

...I'M FINE...

BREAKING THE SPELLS TOOK MORE OUT OF FLICKA THAN I THOUGHT IT WOULD.

THEY MUST'VE BEEN STRONGER THAN I REALIZED, AND SHE SHOULDN'T HAVE AGREED.

I'M GONNA PICK YOU UP NOW, YOU READY?

Wh- don't move her, she's hurt!

HEAVE

HE'LL SURVIVE.

Chapter 3:
Bear Trap

I'D TAKEN LUCAS BACK TO THE DINER, WHERE AUDREY CALLED A COUPLE OF HER SUITS TO PICK THEM UP.

A FEW DAYS LATER, I FOUND A WAD OF BEN FRANKLIN'S IN MY MAIL SLOT.

I HAVEN'T SEEN THEM SINCE.

LOOK, MA, IT'S THE MAN FROM TELEVISION.

MUSHROOM SURPRISE.

IF YOU LIKE MUSHROOMS AND SURPRISES.

SOLD. WITH A COFFEE.

COMING RIGHT UP.

REALLY, NOW? MONEY?

WHAT THE FUCK DOES HE WANT ME TO SAY?

FAME? FORTUNE?

A NICE HUT IN THE ATLANTIS ISLANDS BY THE PALM TREES, FULL OF GIRLS WITH SUN-BLEACHED HAIR AND OLIVE COMPLEXIONS?

REALLY, NOW. MONEY.

AND YET, ACCORDING TO AUDREY, YOU DIDN'T GIVE HER A QUOTE BEFORE YOU TOOK THE JOB.

YOU DIDN'T SEND HER AN INVOICE, EVEN THOUGH SHE GAVE YOU HER CARD.

SOME BUSINESSMAN *YOU* ARE.

HE SOLD ME OUT.

THAT'S IT: I'M NEVER DOING HER NAILS AND BRAIDING HER HAIR EVER AGAIN.

Lucas, did you just rat on me?

I WAS-

HE SANG.

ALL FOR THE GREATER GOOD OF PERSUASION.

Good morning, Colin.

I didn't know how much to pay you. I hope it was enough.

IT WAS.

IT WAS, AND THEN SOME.

I THOUGHT I WAS DONE WITH THE CASE. WHY ARE THEY HERE?

That's great!

If you're satisfied with the amount, then I hope that you'll consider taking another case.

NOT INTERESTED.

MOTHERFUCKERS.

THERE IS NO WAY I'M STICKING MY FOOT BACK INTO THIS BEAR TRAP OF A SITUATION.

AGAIN.

And why not?

You've proven yourself more than capable, what's your excuse this time?

I DON'T WANT TO.

Colin, you realize that you know way more about this than anyone, except for me and Lucas?

Do you really think we'll let you off so easy?

HONESTLY? NO.

......

BUT I'VE ALWAYS BEEN A GLASS-HALF-FULL KIND OF GUY.

...fuck.

chapter 4:
Mongrel

SO, HAVING AN ARM FULL OF SIGILS FEELS A BIT LIKE CONSTANTLY BEING BLED.

WHERE ARE YOURS, THEN?

FORTRESS WEST...

I HOPE I DON'T
RUN INTO ANYONE
WHO RECOGNIZES
ME.

CHAPTER 5:

KEY WEST

FORTRESS WEST

HOME and PRISON
to the Occult of Exodus

THIS IS RATHER ANTI-CLIMATIC.

WHAT DO YOU WANT, A FLYING CARPET?

WHEN I WAS YOUNG I THOUGHT YOU'D NEED MAGIC OR A SPELL TO GET INTO THE FORTRESS.

WHEN I GOT OLDER I THOUGHT YOU'D JUST NEED ENOUGH MONEY.

WELL, IT NEVER OCCURRED TO YOU BEFORE, DID IT?

GOOD POINT.

ONE THING I'VE LEARNED OVER THE YEARS IS THAT PEOPLE DON'T SEE WHAT THEY DON'T WANT TO.

EVEN IF THEY THINK THEY'RE LOOKING FOR IT.

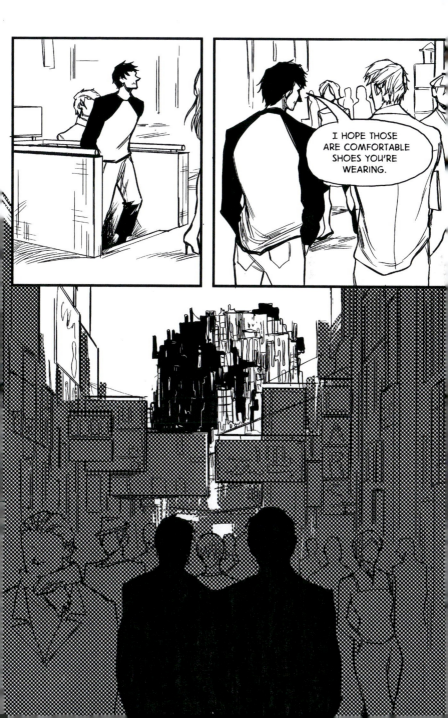

DEAD RAT

...AMONG OTHER IDEALS.

YOU *REALLY* DON'T KNOW ANY OF THIS?

SOME, I DON'T. MOST OF IT I DO. I JUST WANTED YOU TO SAY IT.

......

THE RECTIFIERS FOLLOW THE "STRAIGHT PATH."

PANSHEE AND

AND, SINCE THEY REFUSE TO INTERBREED, THEY'VE RETAINED THEIR ORIGINAL ABILITIES.

IT'S ALL PART OF THEIR BELIEFS THAT THEY FOLLOW TO THE *T*

BASICALLY, THEY'RE ZEALOTS: REALLY STRONG ONES WHO OWN HALF THE FORTRESS.

WE'RE HERE.

chapter 7
COLLOQUIALISMS

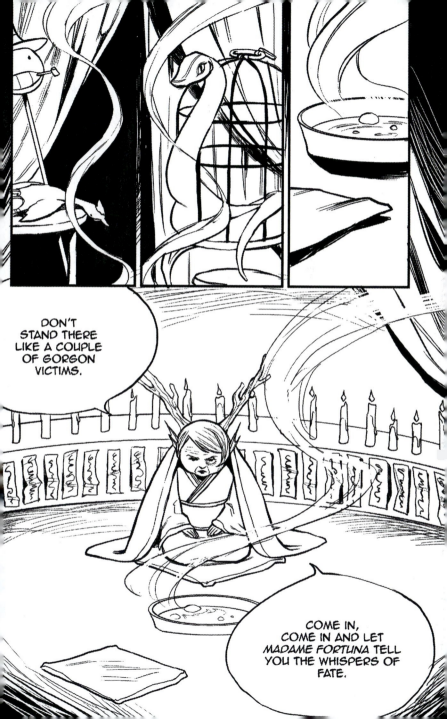

FUN FACT: Audrey's Closet is arranged by degrees of "femme" and "fatale". Then by color.

FUN FACT: Lucas may still be going through puberty.

FLICKA'S PLIGHT:
when Colin makes friends and doesn't show up to work.

JEEZ. WHAT AN OLD-GUY ROOM.

CLANG

Beep!

Might not make it tomorrow either.

TWITCH

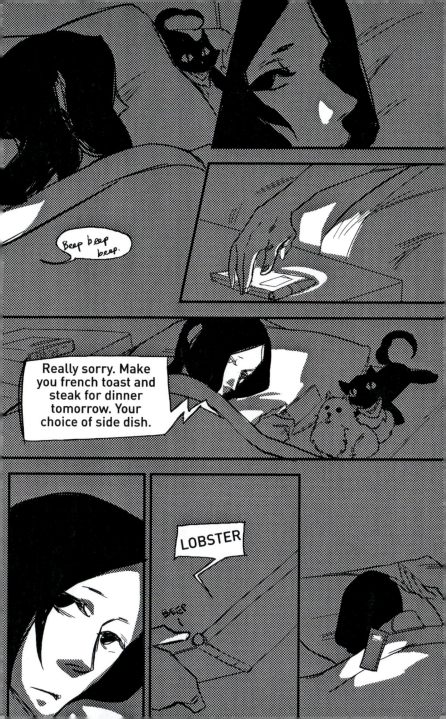

FREETALK:

Chloe: If you've gotten this far in the book, then it must mean that you've read the rest of it (I hope)! Thanks for reading the first volume of **Two Keys**, and we hope it was interesting and fun.

Aliena: Yeah, thanks for sticking with us. I really enjoy this story and I'm glad that Chloe allowed me to work on it. Originally, it was her brain baby alone, but now I have to work hard and try not to drop it on its head too often.

Chloe: This isn't our first book together, but it's probably the first one with a real-ish plot. Although, to be real honest, when I started it I just threw together everything I liked. Which in this case is noir, art deco, big cities, and mysteries. And suits. Not too many of those yet though.

Aliena: Yeah, the story's really changed from it's first inception. I guess we just had to go deeper. Now it's such an interesting world to me, my biggest fear is that I'll assume everyone else sees it as clearly as I do and I'll forget to write something important. Like the fact that Lucas is actually a cow from Jupiter's moon, Io.

Chloe: What a twist! Hopefully we'll have enough information in the story to avoid gaps in knowledge, but if anyone has any questions, you're always super welcome to join us in our forums on *www.mangamagazine.net!*

Aliena: We'd love to hear from you, whether it's questions, answers, questionable answers, or pictures of your cat. So! Until next time, cheers to you all!

—Chloe Chan and Aliena Shoemaker
http://www.new-shoe.com